The Little
Brown Jay

A TALE FROM INDIA

Retold by Elizabeth Claire
Illustrated by Miriam Katin
Folklore Consultant: Bette Bosma

MONDO

MONDO Publishing
980 Avenue of the Americas
New York • NY • 10018

Printed in China

05 06 07 08   9 8

Photograph Credits Scala/Art Resource, NY, Courtesy the Trustees of the British Mu-
seum: p. 17; Craig Lovell/Viesti Associates: p. 18; Photo Shot/Bavaria/Viesti Associates:
p. 19; Will and Deni McIntyre/Photo Researchers: p. 20; Dilip Mehta/Woodfin Camp &
Associates: p. 21 top; S. Nagendra/Photo Researchers: p. 21 bottom.

Library of Congress Cataloging-in-Publication Data

Claire, Elizabeth.
     The little brown jay : a tale from India / retold by Elizabeth Claire ; illustrated by
Miriam Katin.
          p.   cm.
     Summary: A retelling of a traditional Indian tale in which a little bird helps the
beautiful princess Maya through a selfless act of love.
     ISBN 1-879531-17-8 : $21.95. — ISBN 1-879531-44-5 : $9.95. —
ISBN 1-879531-23-2 : $4.95
     [1. Folklore—India. 2. Birds—Folklore.] I. Katin, Miriam, ill. II. Title.
III. Series.
PZ8.1.C49   1994
398.24'528—dc20
[E]   94-14366
                                                                                              CIP
                                                                                              AC

In India I grew up in a large family, and everyone loved to tell me stories. "And then what happened?" I would ask, and a passing grownup would complete the story someone had begun the night before. The tales were full of wonderful explanations of why animals have their special shapes, colors, and habits. Discover for yourself what happens to the little brown jay.

Veena Oldenburg

Once there was a princess named Maya. She was as beautiful and good as the morning sunshine, but her voice was ugly and sharp.

Every day, handsome young Prince Rama rode by Maya's window. Prince Rama never looked at the beautiful princess. He was blind.

"What can I do?" wondered Maya. She was afraid to speak to him in her ugly voice. Rama did not know she was there.

One day, Maya heard a little jay singing in her garden. The jay was a plain brown bird, but its voice was the sweetest in all of India.

Maya began to cry. The jay
stopped singing. "Beautiful lady,
why are you crying?"

"Beauty is nothing to me," said
Maya. "I wish I could sing like you."

"Please don't cry," said the little brown jay. "I will give you my voice."

"But how?" asked Princess Maya.

"At midnight, tonight, go to the lotus pool," said the jay. "Pick the largest lotus flower. Hold it and make your wish."

That night,
the moon was full, and the air
was cold. Maya put on her
beautiful blue silk scarf and
went down to the lotus pool.

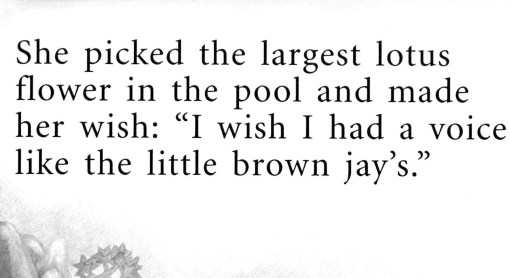

She picked the largest lotus
flower in the pool and made
her wish: "I wish I had a voice
like the little brown jay's."

The magic worked.
Maya began to sing
the sweetest sounds
she had ever heard.
"My wish has come true!"
she cried in her beautiful
new voice.

"I'm glad I could help you," said a sharp voice beside her. It was the little brown jay.

"Oh, thank you! Thank you!" said Maya.

She looked at the jay. "You poor thing, you are shivering from the cold. Let me put my scarf around you."

"I'm warm now," said the jay in his sharp new voice. "And this color is lovely."

"Yes," said Maya. "I wish you could always wear blue."

Instantly, the jay's feathers took the color of the scarf. "Oh, thank you, Princess!"

"Don't thank me," Maya said. "It was the magic lotus flower."

The next day, Prince Rama heard Maya singing. They fell in love and were very happy. Even happier was a beautiful new bird—the little blue jay.

In every part of the world people tell pourquoi (*pur-kwa*), or why, stories to explain why things are the way they are. The story of Princess Maya and the little brown jay is one of these tales from India.

Traditional painting of Indian princess.

Palace gate with towers and pillars.

Pourquoi tales are told in many places. From many South American countries come stories that tell how the sun gave animals their different colors. A tale from Norway answers the question, "Why do bears have stumpy tails?" A Ngoni pourquoi story from Africa tells why monkeys live in trees. And an Aboriginal tale from Australia explains why some birds make their special sounds.

In *The Little Brown Jay*, the pictures show how princesses and princes in India lived more than 300 years ago. Maya lives in a big white palace with tall towers and pillars. Everything is beautifully decorated, even Rama's horse. And the artist decorated the pages with borders showing repeated pictures of objects from the story, such as the magic lotus flower.

Lotus flowers.

India today is a mixture of old and new. In cities, old palaces and temples stand next to modern buildings. Some men wear traditional loose-fitting clothes, and some women wear saris, fabric draped like dresses. Others wear clothes like people in North America.

India's big cities are large and crowded. The streets are full of bicycles, carts, and cars. Some people live in apartments, while others live in small houses

City people wearing traditional and modern clothing.

Painted elephants at a festival.

just outside town. City children go to school, but in many villages children stay home and work with their families.

The people's love of beauty can be seen in their paintings, clothing, and jewelry. Even the elephants people ride at festivals are painted with designs. In villages, local artists paint stories on paper, and people gather to listen to the artists tell their stories.

Artist painting a story picture.